Tito the Tooth:
SUCCESS

by Zully Pina

DORRANCE
PUBLISHING CO
EST. 1920
PITTSBURGH, PENNSYLVANIA 15238

Dorrance Publishing Co
585 Alpha Drive
Suite 103
Pittsburgh, PA 15238
Visit our website at www.dorrancebookstore.com

ISBN: 978-1-6461-0078-1
eISBN: 978-1-6461-0901-2

Tito the Tooth:

SUCCESS

Once upon a time there was a baby tooth who lived in Mouthland.

His name was Tito the tooth.

Tito never left Mouthland.

Tito had many friends. All the teeth in Mouthland were living happily.

They always talked to each other and dreamed about the day the Tooth Fairy would come to bring them to Tooth Fairyland where they would live happily forever.

Mr. Toothbrush, Mr. Toothpaste, and Mr. Dental Floss visited Mouthland two or three times a day after Ms. Meal finished the tooth training. Ms. Meal always brought the teeth's best friends: Fruits, Vegetables, Good Candies, Water, and Vitamins.

Mr. Dentist was the guidance counselor for Mr. Toothpaste, Mr. Toothbrush, and Mr. Dental Floss.

They assisted Mr. Dentist with keeping Mouthland's residents happy and healthy.

Everything was peaceful and happy in Mouthland UNTIL ONE DAY a stranger came to

Mouthland. All the teeth were surprised to see a stranger coming to Mouthland.

They ignored him, but Tito was a friendly tooth and approached the stranger.

"What's your name?" Tito asked.

"My name is Cavity," the stranger said.

"Why are you here?" Tito asked.

"I just came to be around all the teeth in Mouthland. I want to always be with all of you. Can you help me to be around all your tooth friends?" Cavity asked.

"Of course," Tito answered. "C'mon, I will show you around."

Then Tito and Cavity started to walk around Mouthland. Tito was very happy to have a new friend, and he wanted to share him with all his tooth friends.

Tito asked, "How often are you going to visit us?"

"I want to stay forever," Cavity answered.

"Forever?" Tito asked.

"Yes, forever," Cavity answered.

Tito and the other teeth were very happy for the new friend who wanted to live in Mouthland.

Then they started to tell Cavity all about Mouthland.

They wanted Cavity to meet Mr. Toothbrush, Mr. Toothpaste, Mr. Dental Floss,

Ms. Meal, and her friends, Fruits, Vegetables, Vitamins, Water, and Good Candies.

When Tito and his tooth friends told Cavity about all the other friends they had, Cavity started shaking.

"What's wrong?" Tito asked.

"I'm scared," Cavity answered.

"Scared of what?" asked Tito.

"I'm scared of Mr. Toothbrush, Mr. Toothpaste, Mr. Dental Floss, and especially Mr. Dentist."

"Ha ha ha ha ha! You don't have to be scared," Tito said. "Mr. Toothbrush, Mr. Toothpaste, and Mr. Dental Floss are a tooth's best friends. Mr. Dentist is their guidance counselor. They assist Mr. Dentist in all things related to Mouthland," said Tito.

"But I honestly fear them. I don't think they like me," said Cavity.

"They will like you. You don't have to be afraid. Mr. Toothbrush, Mr. Toothpaste, Mr. Dental Floss, and Mr. Dentist are helping all the teeth in Mouthland to be healthy and get ready to move to Tooth Fairyland where we all are going to live happily forever. Ms. Meal and her friends, Fruits, Vegetables, Vitamins, Water, and Good Candies, are also doing their part in our journey to Tooth Fairyland," Tito continued.

"C'mon, Cavity. Come, it is almost time for Mr. Toothbrush, Mr. Toothpaste, and Mr. Dental Floss to come.

Cavity said, "I'm very scared of them. I promise I will try not to be scared."

Then came the time for Mr. Toothbrush, Mr. Toothpaste, and Mr. Dental Floss to come to Mouthland.

All the teeth were happy and excited to see them. They came to greet them.

For the first time, Tito was behind. Mr. Toothbrush, Mr. Toothpaste, and Mr. Dental Floss were surprised Tito wasn't the first to come and greet them.

Meanwhile, Tito was trying to convince Cavity that Mr. Toothbrush, Mr. Toothpaste, and Mr. Dental Floss were good, and there was nothing to be scared about.

Tito told Cavity, "C'mon, Cavity, let's meet them before they go away. I'll show you. Let me go first."

Tito started running to meet with Mr. Toothbrush, Mr. Toothpaste, and Mr. Dental Floss before they left.

Cavity held Tito and said, "Please, Tito, let me hide behind you. I don't want them to see me."

"But why?" Tito asked.

"In time I will explain," Cavity said.

"Okay," said Tito.

By the time Tito came, Mr. Toothbrush, Mr. Toothpaste, and Mr. Dental Floss were already gone.

As the days and nights passed, Tito wasn't able to make it on time to meet with Mr. Toothpaste, Mr. Toothbrush, and Mr. Dental Floss. For any time they came, Cavity hid behind Tito the tooth. All the other teeth in Mouthland were worried about Tito. He wasn't the same happy tooth he always was.

One day Mr. Toothbrush, Mr. Toothpaste, and Mr. Dental Floss asked, "What happened to Tito? We haven't seen him in a while, and it is almost time for him to move to Tooth Fairyland.

There was a silence.

THEN, one of Tito's tooth friends said, "Ever since Cavity came to town, we haven't see Tito around as often, and when we see him, Cavity is always hidden behind him. He is not the same."

"He looks sad," said another of Tito's tooth friends.

"Who did you say is Tito's new friend?" Mr. Toothbrush asked.

"Cavity," they all answered.

"CAVITY?" said Mr. Toothpaste.

"Yes, Cavity," the teeth answered.

"OH NO!" said Mr. Dental Floss. "We have to tell Mr. Dentist.

Then Mr. Toothbrush turned around and said to the rest of the teeth, "You teeth, stay where you are. Do not come close to Tito until we speak to Mr. Dentist. He will know what to do."

All the teeth in town were talking about what Mr. Toothbrush said, and even though they loved Tito, they walked away when Tito tried to say hello, for he was always with Cavity who was hiding behind him.

Mr. Toothbrush, Mr. Toothpaste and Mr. Dental Floss came back to Mouthland. They were looking for Tito. Tito was excited they were looking for him and ran to meet them.

He told Cavity, "My friends Mr. Toothbrush, Mr. Toothpaste, and Mr. Dental Floss are looking for me. Come, Cavity."

Cavity answered, "You go, Tito. I'll hide behind you."

Tito did not say anything else. He just wanted to see his friends. When he was finally in front of them, he couldn't hold his excitement. He ran to hug them. They hugged him back, but they saw something hiding behind him,

"What is that?" Mr. Toothbrush asked.

"This is Cavity, my new friend."

"Really?" said Mr. Toothpaste,

"C'mon, Cavity, don't be scared," said Tito.

Mr. Dental Floss asked, "Why are you shaking, Cavity?"

Cavity just looked at them and then looked down without answering.

Tito said, "Cavity is scared of you and the Fruits and the Vegetables and the Vitamins and the Water and the Good Candies."

Then Mr. Toothbrush said to Tito, "Tito, you have to see Mr. Dentist. He will help you to help Cavity. See, Cavity is always hiding behind you, and you are already starting to get dark spots on you. You are not supposed to have dark spots. That is not good for you. The Tooth Fairy is coming soon to take you to Tooth Fairyland."

Tito look down and asked, "Will having dark spots not allow me to live in Tooth Fairyland happily forever?

"I'm not sure about that, Tito. You have to see Mr. Dentist. He will know, and he will tell you."

As soon as Mr. Toothbrush, Mr. Toothpaste, and Mr. Dental Floss left, Cavity started crying and said, "Tito, don't go to Mr. Dentist. He will separate us, and we will not be friends. Please, Tito. Please, Tito."

"But, Cavity, Ever since you have been hiding behind me, my friends don't come close. The only friend I have is you and Bad Candies, and I got dark spots, and I have started

getting holes on me that hurt. You say that is okay, but I don't feel okay!"

Cavity looked down and quietly hugged Tito.

Meanwhile, Mr. Toothbrush, Mr. Toothpaste, and Mr. Dental Floss received instructions from Mr. Dentist who said, "We are facing a very difficult situation. Cavity hides behind Tito the tooth and doesn't want to leave. He is bringing Bad Candies with him. This is not good for Tito the tooth, and Bad Candies will bring more of Cavity's relatives to Mouthland. Then all the teeth in Mouthland will have a cavity hiding behind them."

"It is our duty to protect all the teeth. This is what needs to be done. Mr. Toothbrush and Mr. Toothpaste, you will work together. Your duty is to visit Mouthland after every time Ms. Meal goes in. This means at least three times a day. Mr. Dental Floss, you are to visit between the teeth at least two times a day. I, Mr. Dentist, will be sure to go to Mouthland at least once a year. Can I count on you, team?"

"YES!" they answered at once.

Meanwhile, Tito was starting to get more dark spots, and what was worse, he started to get small, dark holes all over due to the fact he was becoming close friends with Cavity's best friend, Bad Candies.

The rest of Mouthland started to get the same way. Cavity sneaked in her relatives and his friend Bad Candies' relatives. Cavity and his friends were taking over Mouthland.

OR AT LEAST THEY THOUGHT.

They didn't know Mr. Toothbrush, Mr. Toothpaste, and Mr. Dental Floss were on the way to save Tito and all the teeth in Mouthland. They had all of Mr. Dentist's instructions about what to do.

Mr. Toothbrush, Mr. Toothpaste, and Mr. Dental Floss arrived to Mouthland. They were on a mission.

All the sudden, out of nowhere, they encountered Cavity and some of his and Bad Candies' relatives.

Cavity yelled at them, "Get out! For we have taken over Mouthland. You have no business here!"

Tito was surprised! Cavity was supposed to be good.

Then Tito said, "Cavity, they are our friends, and you are supposed to be good. What happened to you?"

"Stay away, Tito! You belong with us!" said Cavity.

"Not so fast! For we are here to protect Mouthland!" said Mr. Toothbrush.

Cavity and his relatives and Bad Candies put up a big fight.

Mr. Toothbrush, Mr. Toothpaste, and Mr. Dental Floss started to lose strength when all of a sudden they heard a

voice saying, "I'm here to save Mouthland with you, Mr. Toothbrush, Mr. Toothpaste, and Mr. Dental Floss! We are a team!"

It was Mr. Dentist!

Cavity, Bad Candies, and their relatives were so scared. They had no other choice but to run and leave Mouthland forever.

Tito was very confused.

Then Mr. Toothbrush, Mr. Toothpaste, and Mr. Dental Floss explained to Tito that Cavity brought his relatives and Bad Candies to become stronger and to cause pain in Mouthland.

They advised Tito to stay away from them if he ever wanted to go with the Tooth Fairy and live happily ever after in Tooth Fairyland.

As the time went by, Tito and all the teeth in Mouthland recovered the happiness that was theirs.

Then the day Tito was anxiously waiting for finally arrived.

The Tooth Fairy came to take Tito to Tooth Fairyland to live happily ever after.

Tito was so happy, but at the same time he was sad, for he was leaving his friends behind.

The Tooth Fairy told him, "Tito, don't be sad. They are also coming when the time is right, and all of you will be together again."

"But what if cavity and the Bad Candies come?"

Then Mr. Toothbrush, Mr. Toothpaste, Mr. Dental Floss, and Mr. Dentist who had come to say goodbye to Tito said, "Don't worry, Tito! We are here to protect Mouthland!"

Then Tito and the Tooth Fairy left together. Tito waved bye-bye as he was leaving, and Mr. Toothbrush, Mr. Toothpaste, Mr. Dental Floss, Mr. Dentist, and all the residents of Mouthland waved bye-bye too.

*The character of the Tooth Fairy Godmother was inspired
by my granddaughter, Alexandria Isabella Fernandez*

CPSIA information can be obtained
at www.ICGtesting.com
Printed in the USA
LVHW071548270321
682641LV00002B/20